T0354338

A WOMAN'S
TRAIT LIES
IN HER EYES

A WOMAN'S TRAIT LIES IN HER EYES

AUGIE BRUNO

ARCHWAY
PUBLISHING

Archway Publishing books may be ordered through booksellers or by contacting:

Archway Publishing
1663 Liberty Drive
Bloomington, IN 47403
www.archwaypublishing.com
844-669-3957

Interior Image Credit: Augie Bruno

ISBN: 978-1-6657-6162-8 (sc)
ISBN: 978-1-6657-6163-5 (e)

Library of Congress Control Number: 2024912156

Print information available on the last page.

Archway Publishing rev. date: 06/21/2024

CHAPTER 1

My story begins on a typical cold Saturday night in February. Snow was falling and the wind was howling. I was sixteen and two months pregnant. My parents were starting to notice that something was different about me. As usual, my father was drunk and was ordering my mother to serve his every need. I watched as he sat with his bottle of Jack Daniels which he sipped continuously as he smoked one cigarette after another. He already came home drunk after drinking all day at the local tavern. In between serving my father, my mother cleaned the house and prepared food for dinner. I was struggling on how to tell my parents of my predicament. My father would never understand how I could allow this to happen. My mother would agree with my father no matter how he reacted. In my mother's life she was expected to take care of the children, cook and clean the home. My father was expected to work and support the family. I did not mention my predicament because I wanted to wait for a time when my father was sober. I realized this would not happen.

On Sunday I called my sister Gail and asked her if she would pick me up. I told her I needed to talk to her alone and tell her something important. This would be an unusual event because our family never got together on Sunday. I told her to pick me up on the corner of the street at 1:30pm. The chill of winter made me cold as I waited for her to pick me up. As I stood there shivering, I began to think what I would tell my sister. As her vehicle turned the corner, I began to get cold feet about telling her I was pregnant. As I climbed in her vehicle, Gail smiled and asked where I wanted to go. As we rode in the vehicle, I began to think she was very much like our father. She was controlling and a take charge person that would take great pride in scolding me. Gail always had to get the last word in. She was a plotter, schemer and would do anything for money. She would later prove this to me as she got older. But at this time, she was the only lifeline I had. We stopped at Deny's Restaurant and asked for the corner booth. My sister, as usual, had to spend endless time reviewing the menu. I was extremely nervous and impatient with her as she read every line. She also had an annoying hum as she reviewed the selections. After five minutes, which felt like an hour, she said what's up. Pappa picking on you or is mom's cooking giving you indigestion? I questioned whether I wanted to tell her. Then I thought I would blame my father for mistreating me and how unhappy my childhood was, and I relied on boys to comfort me.

All at once I felt relieved that really this was not my fault at all, and she would help me because she did not like our parents.

I then thought how to tell her in a way she would understand. But I had to make sure that Gail felt the same way as I did. She moved out of my parents' home when she was seventeen because of the situation with our father. Father would ridicule her about her

looks and make derogatory remarks about her being overweight. I had to admit she did look a little dumpy and father was a womanizer that liked pretty women. Gail did not fit under that umbrella. Gail resented this treatment from our father, and she compensated by trying to control everyone's life.

I started out telling Gail that father was drinking heavily, and mother was sticking up for him. He was punishing me like he punished you. He also had that stupid bell which he used to summon mother or me to serve is every need. Since you left, he has taken his unhappiness out on mother and me. I noticed a smile began to form on Gail's face. I also noticed it was some kind of redemption for her. She also got this motherly look as if this is what she needed to fulfil her life. She then asked how she could help. I then blurted out that I was pregnant, I said it so loud, everybody's head turned around in the restaurant. Gail was stunned, speechless and senseless. She blurted out how this could happen and who is the father? Just let me know who the father is, and I will take care of him. That jerk is going to pay. You poor child.

What a relief, she was on my side. Now I needed to tell the truth that I could not be sure who the father was. This would be difficult unless I expanded my story slightly. Gail, you know how loneliness can drive a person to do strange things. Gail said, "What do you mean. You know how father controlled us and forced us to serve. Gail, "I transferred that upbringing to serve many boys". As tears rolled down my eyes, I noticed Gail began to cry. I said, "we lived terrible lives". Gail said" I am here to help".

CHAPTER 2

The following days were cold and windy. My life was in a tailspin at school and at home. I was extremely depressed and scared. I did not know how to tell my parents that I was two months pregnant. They could never understand how their daughter would be so stupid. There was nothing I could dream up that would explain my pregnancy. I decided to call Gail and ask her if she could help me. I called and asked her what she was doing. Gail said I am talking to you. This was typical of Gail; she always had a way of cutting me short to get to the facts. She asked whether I told our parents? I told her no because I was having trouble coming up with a story. Gail said, "forget the story and tell them the truth". I cannot tell them; you know how they are. Gail, "please help me". Gail said, "let me think about it and I will get back to you in a few days".

As the days went by, my clothes were getting tighter, and mother made a remark about me going on a diet. I laughed and told her that I was going to start working out next week. Somehow this pleased her, and she went about her household duties cleaning up after my father. That evening, Gail called to talk to me. She said Lee, let's get together on Saturday at the mall and I will lay out a plan. I asked when, and as usual she told me she did not have the time. That was two days from now and the anxiety was killing me. I just wanted to know what her plan was, the anxiety was killing me.

Saturday, I woke up and I was not feeling well. I think this may be the start of morning sickness which I learned about in a class at school. I was looking forward to meeting Gail to talk about how I was going to tell my parents. We met at noon and of course Gail had to eat and never enjoyed talking while she ate. I was dying of suspense waiting for her to tell me what the plan was. She finally took the last bite of food and proceeded to tell me that our father will ask you to move out. She went on to say she would invite our parents to her house for dinner and I would proceed to tell them the truth about me being two months pregnant.

The day came and Gail prepared a wonderful dinner with all the trimmings. Everyone was quiet at the table occasionally glancing at each other. After dessert was served, Gail announced I had something to tell them. Gail stared at me, and I was frozen in my seat. I was struggling to get the words out. Finally, I blurted out I was two months pregnant. My father stared at me and if looks could kill, I would be laying the floor gasping for breath. He stood up and told my mother to get their coats. This would be the first time I witnessed him leaving a half glass of liquor. As he opened the door, he turned around and said, get out of my house. I finally realized my sister was exceptionally smart asking me to pack my clothes before I came to her house for dinner.

Here I was the next day living in my sister's house pregnant, with no money and emotionally upset. Although I felt relieved after telling my parents, it did little to help my situation. Gail went to get my clothes at my parents' house, which she found on the front lawn. Maybe I did not deserve better treatment from my parents, then again, I had let them down. At this time in my life, I needed to find out what type of women I wanted to be. Like Gail's self- confident ways or my mother's lack of self-respect. The first thing I needed to do was to figure out how to be a mother.

I was fortunate because my sister lived walking distance from the school. I could go and come home from school without interrupting her work schedule. I dreaded going to school wearing maternity clothes when the time came. I had three months of school left in this school year which I could wear loose fitting clothes. I would not be so lucky in my senior year.

During this time, I learned to respect Gail for her achievements in life. She earned a college degree and had an accounting job at a big company. She had a nice apartment and new vehicle. Although she had few friends and no boyfriend, she did seem happy.

Gail took me to the doctor to make sure I had no issues with my pregnancy. The doctor told us everything seemed to be okay. He asked if we wanted to know if it was a girl or boy. I told him not at his time. The morning sicknesses had gotten worse which caused me to be late for school and miss occasionally. My grades were dropping, and my teachers were getting suspicious. I was making excuses about having an infection and was seeing a doctor. I had only two more months left in this school year.

On Wednesday morning, I woke up with severe pain in my pelvic area and bleeding. I was not feeling well, and I was burning up. I called Gail at work and told her I needed help. She came home and took me to the emergency room, and they diagnosed me as having a miscarriage. I was heartbroken and sad at what had happened. I was going to be seventeen in two months and had lost my child. This was later confirmed at the doctor's office. The ride home from the doctor's office was quiet with few words spoken. Gail asked if I wanted to let our parents know. I told her I had no interest in talking to or seeing them. Gail suggested we stop for lunch and talk about the future. I agreed it was time to plan my life moving forward.

When I was a child, I dreamed of being a tall woman, thinly built like the models in perfume commercials. They were beautiful and scantily dressed and, in many cases, they were escorted with handsome men. In other commercials women were cleaning their house or making dinners. I was at a loss of the different traits of women. One day I would decide what trait I wanted to be.

Going to school when not pregnant made a big difference. I fantasized that teachers and my fellow students were always watching me. I may have been too sensitive thinking they were. I was waiting for the school year to end and get a job. I needed to find my place on this earth. To begin with, what gender roles or stereotypes would I decide on. I wanted to be liked and accomplished like my sister Gail. I needed to go to college and get a degree and also support myself. I knew I would be tested all my life and maybe questioned about my previous mistakes I made.

CHAPTER 3

I was near graduation from high school, and I had applied to colleges in my local area. I got accepted at a community college that was offering a small scholarship in psychology. It wasn't much but every little bit would help. If I worked at my job and if Gail would allow me to live free at her apartment, I could make it.

Gail met an older man she seemed to like. This is good for Gail because she likes a man with money. He is spending more time at the apartment, and they are holding hands on the couch. In fact, they remind me of two children. I watched this relationship grow because they loved each other. Finally, a year later they were married and kept the apartment and an ocean front condo in Florida. I started college the following year and worked hard to keep my scholarship. I started in general business which taught me how to budget money and understand financial terms.

I met a lot of nice people in my classes and enjoyed their company. There was one person that stood out. He was quiet and reserved and somewhat unapproachable. He also had a smile which attracted people. I introduced myself and told him my name was Lee and he told me his name was Paul. I told him we needed to get together and talk about the classes we were taking. I was not sure he ever gave me an answer. However, I did make a comment that I liked him and hoped he would not get mad at me.

I walked away thinking why did I say that? I thought maybe I was a woman that wanted to communicate her feelings freely. Maybe this is the positive character I want to be. I wanted so much to not fall into a stereotype that would destroy my life. I saw this firsthand with my own mother. My first thought was he would never talk to me again. However, the next day he did talk to me. He even asked me to join him to have a cup of coffee.

At this time, I was only interested in my career and the study of women's character traits. These traits are numerous which include nurturing, faithful, kindness, strong willed, patience, humor and confidence. There had to be a better way of characterizing these traits by using actual examples. I set out to get a better understanding of how I could actually see these traits in action.

I started with my friends, but they were students and did not have a lot of experience. I contacted a young man named Tony that supported me through my pregnancy. His father was an unusual person with a superior education, and I was told he had numerous experiences with people. The only problem was some people in the neighborhood called him the Godfather and some referred to him as ex-CIA and some people just called him Dan.

I remember asking my friend about him but never got a clear answer what his father did for a living. I decided to talk to him and ask him for his help. I met with him the following week and was taken back that he was no one you wanted to cross. He told me he wanted to think about my request, but I felt he was stalling to do some background check on me. During that short meeting with him, I felt he was the most interesting person I had ever met. He called me two days later and told me he would help me out as much as he could. I was delighted because he knew more than he was telling me. We decided to meet the following week and discuss what I expected from him.

The first meeting was awkward because everything I asked him, he refused to answer. Which caused me to ask more questions about his personal life. Finally, he said in a blunt manner that my research was about women and not him. He asked me where I wanted to start on Women's traits?

My first thought was to bring up the slang word Bag Lady. I also ask him what he thought were the most important traits a woman could have. He told me the slang words meant a homeless woman who carried her possessions in a bag. This was derived from stereotypes of men and women. The man was expected to be the bread earner and the woman was expected to maintain the home and raise the children. The concern was if something happened to the bread earner the women would be helpless. Some people have said this is a concern of fifty percent of the women today.

To address your question on the most important traits of women, I would tell you that my analysis may be different than other professionals. The study of traits always brings up whether a person can change a trait. In my opinion, a trait starts with the eyes. You can change your looks, your speech, your ideology but it all starts with the eyes because that cannot be changed. In simple terms you are not likely to select a trait. Although there are numerous traits, I think the five most important ones are social skills, self-awareness, humor, empathy and motivation. I will try to explain these traits in more detail, and you can take notes for the paper you are writing for school.

1. Social Skills. The person is a good listener and communicates feelings. This is most noticeable when the person asks questions and explains their feelings in detail.
2. Self-awareness'. This person shows self-confidence and projects positive feelings.
3. Humor. Healthy humor and projects openness to change and challenges. This can be characterized by not spending time on mistakes but always looking to the future.
4. Empathy. The person accepts flaws and looks for the better in people. May even try to help a person in need.
5. Motivation. Goal orientated and Try's to live a happier life. Strives for better results in the challenges of life.

He also told me the most interesting trait was about some women that had an attraction to gangsters. He said gangsters care about their community and live by their own rules that include honor and conduct. He thought more research should be done on this trait. He also mentioned a myth about old maid concerns. He thought that was a lot of garbage.

I was taken back by the traits he had picked that were the most important. The traits he mentioned impacted me personally. I was trying to pick a trait for my life to make sure I did not make any future mistakes. I wanted to race home to look in the mirror to see what trait I possessed. I wanted to see what my eyes would tell me.

Before I left, he told me he did not want to be quoted in my paper and if the five traits meant something to me, I should do further research on them. I thanked him and left. I hoped this would not be the last time I would see him. As I was riding home on the bus, I thought to myself I knew nothing more about this man than the first time I met him.

I finished my paper with a smile on my face. I thought I did an excellent job. Every time I proofread the paper; I would think of the time I spent with my friend's father talking about traits. He was so easy to listen to and talk to. I wished he was my father. I did get an A on the paper and the teacher wrote a note on the paper that I should consider being a writer.

CHAPTER 4

I returned to school to start my second year. I was tired because I worked two jobs all summer to save enough money for tuition and books. I would put my earnings from my second job in the bank to use for courses and books.

I was excited because I would be taking courses that were more relative to what I wanted to be. I also saw my friend Tony and told him how much his father helped with my paper. I told him how lucky he was to have such a great father. I also told him how impressed I was with his knowledge and asked what he does for a living. I never got an answer. I guess the apple does not fall far from the tree. He did mention a party at his father's home the following Saturday and asked me if I wanted to go. Of course, I said yes.

The following Saturday Tony picked me up in a beautiful red sports car. I told him what a nice car. He told me it was his father's. I wore one of my sister's dresses and high heel shoes. When we arrived, there were vehicles parked in a straight line in front of the house. When entering the house, we were greeted by a young man offering to take our coats. There were about fifty people at the party with the men in suits and tie and the women in beautiful dresses. There were a few couples dancing, but most were talking. There were hostesses offering all kinds of food and drinks. I was introduced to a few of his relatives and friends of his father. His father walked over and thanked me for coming and asked me how I did at school with the paper. I told him I got an A and thanked him for his help. Then he said the funniest thing. He asked me what my eyes told me when I looked in the mirror and he walked away. I would spend days thinking about that question. Then it occurred to me he knew more about me than I told him.

I knew this school year was going to be exciting and I needed to work real hard on the traits I wrote in my paper and expand the list. I was aware I could not pick a trait to transition into. So, I had to deal with what I knew about myself. I also knew it was difficult to evaluate oneself. I started to review statistics from big cities where approximately twenty-six % of women live alone. This could be why bag lady was talked about so much. I started to date a little, but I was shy due to my previous pregnancy. Somehow, I developed a mental block and developed a shyness toward men. I just did not want to get involved.

I ran into Paul, and we talked about the classes we were taking and if we were dating anyone. He asked me to go to his family's annual fall party. I accepted because I had not been around my family in a long time.

He picked me up and we drove for about thirty minutes to arrive at this exclusive neighborhood with large mansions and manicured lawns. I was speechless because I had never seen homes like this. As we entered the house I was taken back by the size of the rooms and the number of people at the party. I never expected my friend would live in such a beautiful home. We chatted and he introduced me to his father and mother and two sisters. I noticed a few tough looking guys at the party that were watching everybody with stern looks on their faces. I asked my friend who they were, and he said they work for his father.

Everything was fantastic from the shrimp to the caviar. I was not from this world, but I was enthused about the house, the people and the food. I did notice there seemed to be a lot of young women with older men. I was looking around the room when I spotted a man in the corner. He turned slightly and I recognized Dan talking to two ladies. This was the man that helped me with my school paper. I asked my friend about Dan, and he gave me a funny look and he never answered the question. I never talked to Dan that evening, but I could not get him out of my mind. We left the party, and I knew not to ask any questions.

On the way home I began to remember what he told me about women that like gangsters. He did not think it was a separate trait but would fall under empathy. He spent very little time talking about the subject because it seemed to bother him. Somehow, I was attracted to this subject because of my dealings with Dan and the party I was at. Maybe because everything was a secret. I went to the library to do some research on women that were attracted to gangsters. Although there is reading material, I found very little about a woman's attraction to gangsters. For example, what was Bonnie's attraction to Clyde?

As time went on, Gail spent more time in Florida with her husband. I had not talked to my parents in three years. I was getting a little lonely in the apartment alone. I finally realized how widows have a tough time fighting off loneliness. I started to think I needed to date a little and find more friends to get out of the apartment. This was not easy for me because I did not have a lot of money to spend or have a good feeling about men.

I also thought about donating my time to a good cause but realized I did not have a lot of time after working and studying. I decided to spend extra time on my homework and leave the self-pity for another day. Just as I was sitting down at the desk, Paul called me and asked me if I wanted to go for a ride. He said he needed to drop off a package. I told him I would be ready in about twenty minutes. As he drove, we talked about school and the classes we were taking. We arrived at this night club, and he grabbed the package, and we went inside. I was taken back by the women in the place and the gangster looking guys. The cigar smoke was so thick my eyes were bothering me. His father took the package and said hello to me and gave his son a look that scared me. I think this was a sign for us to leave. On the way back he suggested we stop at a local hamburger place and talk a little. He knew my wheels were turning and I had a million questions. As we had a milk shake and a burger, I blurted out what is that place and why did your father give you such a dirty look. He did not say anything like he was programed only to say certain things. Again, like at his parents' party he said nothing, and I was left with unanswered questions. He dropped me off at home and

I sat on the couch thinking there must be something wrong with me. Why was everyone so secretive?

I was looking forward to completing the school year and spending time enjoying the summer. My grades were excellent, and I met a lot of nice people that I became friends with. As always, we all agreed to meet on a regular basis. We only got together a couple of times because everyone was busy. I would only see Gail a few times during the summer. She would complement me about how well I was maintaining the apartment. She would also ask me the same question whether I talked to our parents when She knew the answer because she talked to our parents all the time. Paul would call me once in a while and we would discuss what we were doing during summer break. He was the same mysterious guy that had the ability only to tell you certain things. This was not the basis of good friendship. He asked me out a few times and I made the excuse I was busy. I had the feeling he did not believe me.

CHAPTER 5

Fall arrived and I was back in school. This would be Junior year to get the classes that would impact my future. I would spend considerable time in the library researching homework assignments. It was good to see my friends and tell each other what we did all summer. Their stories were so exciting telling me about the trips they took with their families and the cookouts at the beach. It all sounded so wonderful to see my friends spending time with their families. Unfortunately, I had little to say about my summer. I do not think anyone would be interested in my workplace experiences.

I was walking down the hall, and a fellow student ran into me, and my books fell on the floor. He immediately apologized and then helped me pick up my books. When we were standing face to face, I noticed he had a Kippah on his head. It was a wonderful blue. He introduced himself as Joel and asked me what my name was. I told him my name was Lee. A few days later I ran into Joel in the cafeteria. I was sitting alone, and he asked if he could sit in the vacant chair. I asked him what he was studying to be, and he said a heart doctor. I thought that was unusual because this was a community college. Most students studying to be a doctor either go to Harvard or Yale. After my lunch, I went to class. The following week I was in the cafeteria and ran into Joel. I needed to ask him why he was going to a community college wanting to be a doctor. He explained his mother was ill and he wanted to be near her and that it was not possible to be in Boston. He said his brother was graduating from Harvard and was going to be a lung doctor. He said there was going to be a family celebration for his brother at their home. He then asked me if I wanted to go to the party. I told him I would love to attend. He said he would pick me Saturday at 6:00pm and I gave Him my address and telephone number.

Saturday came and Joel picked me up and even opened the car door for me. When we arrived at home, it was well lit and had signs saying Happy Graduation. Inside there were approximately twenty-five people. All the men were wearing Kippah's and there was a woman in a wheelchair. Joel introduced me to his mother that was in the wheelchair, and we went to each person he introduced me as his friend from college. There had to be at least fifteen doctors between the men and women. It was doctor this and that. I thought if I had a heart attack this would be the perfect place. Each person made an effort to talk to me. The door opened and his brother came into the room, and everybody toasted him using the title Dr Robert Ellner. Although his brother was older, they looked alike. I kept thinking Joel would walk through that door one day he would be toasted as Dr Joel Ellner. This was not like the other parties I went to where there seemed to be secrets.

Every question I asked was answered in detail. On the way home I told Joel he had a wonderful family and he asked me about mine. I dodged the question and hoped we would be home in a few minutes. I could not think of an answer that would make sense.

Paul called to invite me to his parents' annual party. I told him I would get back to him because I needed to look at my schedule. After some thought, I could see Dan again and I would definitely enjoy a night out. The rest of the evening I was thinking about the people at the party and the food. I saw Paul the next day at school and told him I would go. I promised myself I would ask questions and get answers. I was intrigued about these people. Maybe I was one of those women that Dan mentioned that admired gangsters.

I was excited waiting for the night to arrive and decided to have my hair and nails done. When we arrived at the party I was introduced to politicians, doctors and a priest. I thought this was very unusual and somewhat disturbing. I also noticed Paul was treated as royalty. As I looked around at the guests, I spotted Dan with a group of men. I waited patiently until he was alone, and I walked up to him to say hello. He remembered me and asked me how school was going. I told him I was doing very well, and I had some questions I wanted to ask him. He had a funny look on his face and commented that this was not the place to ask questions.

I pushed hard for a meeting with him and after about a minute, he said call me and he slowly walked away. I went back to Paul, and he offered me some wine. The evening was marvelous, and the food was fantastic. I asked Paul where the lady's room was, and he pointed to this hallway. As I entered, there was a young lady my age standing in front of the mirror. She made a comment to me how lucky I was to be escorted by the boss's son. I immediately asked who she was escorted by, and she gave me a name which I thought was nickname. As we were riding home, Paul finally asked me why I was so interested in Dan. This had to be the first time Paul would ask me a question pertaining to the party. I told him Dan had helped me with my paper on women's traits for a school paper and I wanted to ask him some questions about what he told me. Paul said, "be careful what you ask" and dropped me off at the apartment. Was this a warning or just a friendly recommendation?

The following week I called Dan to set up a meeting with him. We decided to meet the following week on Wednesday at noon at his home. I would spend this time to accumulate notes on subjects I wanted to ask him. I went through a lot of notes and discarded half of them. I knew for sure this was going to be a challenge. He guarded his statements more than anyone I met before. I needed to come up with a solid excuse to ask these questions. I went to bed thinking I could find a reason tomorrow. I woke up and it hit me like a ton of bricks. I would tell him I was thinking about writing a book about women and their traits.

As I was riding on the bus to Dan's home, I began to get cold feet on the questions I would ask him. When I arrived, a gray-haired woman answered door and ask if I was Lee. I introduced myself and she escorted me to the dining room. Dan was at the table and asked me to have lunch with him. I noticed Dan in the light of day, he had aged from the first time I met him. We had soup and a sandwich and then went to the study. I had never been in this room before. The bookshelves were filled with books and nicknacks. He asked me to sit in a chair and proceeded to ask me why I wanted to meet with him. I told him I was considering writing a book about gangsters and their women. He looked at me with a puzzled look on his face. Then he reminded me when we first met that the high school paper was not about him but about women traits.

I then said, "Dan you are most interesting person I ever met" and somehow there had to be a story about you. I do not want to pry into your personal life, but I have never witnessed such knowledge, parties and secrets before. Dan looked at her and said, "my life is a secret and if I tell you, it is no longer a secret". I am going to ask you to leave to go home and come up with three questions you want to ask me. When you figure out what those questions are, call me and we can discuss them.

I was thinking on the way home what three questions I could ask. What did I really want to know about Dan and why it was so important to me? Was I that woman that was intrigued by gangsters? When I arrived home, I was confused and tired thinking about those three questions. I took a piece of paper and wrote Likely and Not Likely on the top of the page. The questions I would ask: Like are you in the mob? Are you in the CIA or FBI? Dan would never answer those questions. I had to settle on questions like: How do you know so much about women? Why do women like gangster movies? Have you ever written a book? I think these are safe questions and I think Dan will address them. In the following week, I called Dan to set up a meeting with him. He told me next week on Tuesday at noon would work. On the bus going to meet Dan made me a little nervous. I thought maybe he would ignore the questions and ask me to leave. The same lady answered the door and took me to the dining room. Dan asked me if I was hungry, and I said politely no. We went into the library and Dan asked what my questions were. I said in a nervous fashion: "how do you know so much about women"? He said he had spent a lifetime studying people's habits, mannerism and skills. I asked if he was the author of books? He looked at me for a minute and rose out of the chair and went to the bookcase and pulled out a book.

He handed the book to me with a title 'All About Women Traits". I noticed I did not recognize the author's name. He told me he writes books under an assumed name. The final question was why women like gangster movies? Dan told me because those type movies are out of the ordinary which causes a level of excitement. Movies like Little Caeser, Mafioso and Scarface told the story of a crime family that treated crime as something positive, interesting and had different characters. The funny thing is, I have seen those three movies at least two times.

Once again on the bus going home, I was more confused than ever. Dan was an author that attended parties given by gangsters. Somehow there was a missing piece to the puzzle.

CHAPTER 6

Another school year ended, and I was back to work at my two jobs. I had little time to enjoy the summer due to the hours I had to work. My friends mostly did not work because their parents were paying the bills. Paul would call me once in a while to see how I was doing, and Joel asked me to go to dinner a month later.

I would always think of the difference between them. I think one came from a crime family, while the other came from a family of doctors. Paul interested me the most because of his family. The only trouble with Paul, I could not get him to tell me anything about his family. Who has bodyguards and friends like Dan, politicians and judges. So many unanswered questions and thoughts I will never figure out. I was proud of myself because I got straight A in all my classes. If I could do that in my senior year, I would graduate Maga Cum laude.

I would spend most of my time in the library studying and trying to figure out what I would do after graduation. I know Gail would most likely want to give up the apartment. So, I would need a

place to live. As I sat in the library there was this handsome boy staring at me. He had black hair and blue eyes. I tried to ignore his look, but it was difficult. As I sat there, he started walking toward me and introduced himself as Nick and proceeded to ask me what my name was. I told him my name was Lee. He asked if he could sit at the table. I agreed and we began to talk about school and the classes we had taken.

It was almost like love at first sight. He proceeded to ask me out to go to a movie. I agreed in two seconds, and he asked me for my address and telephone number. This was the beginning of a wonderful friendship. We were inseparable through the school year.

Graduation was in sight, and I had maintained my A status. We all received a memo on the number of seats we needed for the graduation ceremony. I put two down because I had asked Gail and her husband to attend. The ceremony was on a hot day outside the college. There were at least three speakers and then the names of those students that achieved Maga Cum Laud status. When my name was announced I stood up and people clapped. What a wonderful feeling. The diplomas were handed out by the Dean, and we left the area to where the guests were. I saw Gail and her husband and a couple behind them. The man I could hardly recognize. It was my father and mother on his side. He looked like he did before he started drinking. My father and mother hugged me and told me how proud they were of me. We went to a restaurant, and everyone apologized for their actions. We were now back as a family five years later.

I think that everybody could change and make a difference in their life. I was an example as well as my father. We both had issues to overcome to move forward. I started the interview process for positions in schools and the corporate world. Although I did not have a teacher's certificate, I could use my psychology degree to open a few doors. I did finally land a job at a high school as an English teacher.

I would see Nick on occasions, and we would go to see shows at the theater. I enjoyed being with him because he made me laugh. Nick could take the simplest things in life and create a wonderful story. He was fun to be with and he always made a fuss over me. Paul would also call, and we would talk forever. The only problem with Paul was that he was too guarded in what he would tell me. He would frustrate me every time I mentioned his parents. I finally lost it one day and shouted, "is your father in the mob"? Once again, I never received an answer. That was the last time Paul, and I would talk to each other.

Nick and I were growing closer together. I was excited to hear from him and if I did not, I would be upset. He also got a job at an engineering company working in their personnel department. He was happy working for the company and would tell me funny things that would happen. He finally asked me to meet his parents and siblings at a dinner prepared by his mother. They were a wonderful family, I received a call from Joel. He told me his mother had passed and he was heading to Harvard Medical School. He was going to be a doctor like his brother and father. He thanked me for being such a nice friend. I told him what I was doing, and he congratulated me on my success. Joel was such a nice person, and I knew he would become a wonderful doctor. Gail was in town with her husband and my parents were going to have us over for dinner. I called my mother and asked her if I could bring a friend. She was delighted when she found out it was a man. I called Nick and invited him to dinner. He was delighted and asked me if he could bring anything. I told him no. Well, he did bring a flower arrangement for my mother. My family loved him, especially my father. I thought it was unusual because they were like salt and pepper. Nick loved my family and said the food was fantastic.

Nick and I were spending more time with each other, and I was getting concerned about telling him about my past. Once again, I needed Gail's assistance while she was still in town. We met at lunch, and I told her what my problem was and if she had any ideas. She asked me if I loved Nick and how I thought Nick felt. I told her I felt we were in love with each other. Gail said what is the problem? I waited a second and said, "should I tell Nick about the Pregnancy"? Gail looked at me and commented that you cannot have a relationship if it starts out with secrets. Tell him and let the chips fall where they fall. If he loves you, he will understand.

CHAPTER 7

I woke up with a headache and heard the winds blowing outside. As I looked out the window the streets were snow covered. I needed to look for a place to live but today was not a good day. I know Gail wanted to close the apartment because the lease was coming up to be renewed. I thought maybe I could lease the apartment but after looking at the new lease, I did not make enough money unless I got a second job. I needed to find a onebedroom apartment in the same neighborhood. I discussed my dilemma with Nick, and he suggested I get a roommate or move to another neighborhood. Somehow, I was thinking he was talking about himself as a roommate.

My most pressing issue is how to tell Nick about my previous pregnancy. I needed to tell him before this relationship would mature any further. I needed to tell him the truth about everything including all the things I did. I decided the best way was to invite him over to my apartment and tell him the whole story. I would hate to lose him, but he may find out one way or another.

I called Nick the next day and invited him over on Saturday night for dinner. He told me he would come but it had to be a little later than I asked. I was nervous all week because I loved Nick and did not want to lose him. Saturday came and I made lasagna with a salad. After dinner Nick asked whether we should watch TV or go rent a movie. I told him I needed to talk to him and tell him something very private. We sat in the front room, and I told him about my childhood living with an alcoholic father and how I was always verbally abused. I could see in his eyes he was holding back tears for my misfortune. I then told him I was turning to the outside for affection from boys that I knew, and I got pregnant at sixteen years old. I could see from his facial expression that he was in shock. He slowly got up from the chair and left the apartment saying good night. I started to cry, and I did not stop until the following morning. The next five days I heard nothing from Nick. I could not sleep at night and when I went to work, the teacher I was shadowing told me to go home because I looked terrible.

On Friday night the phone rang, and it was Nick on the line. He said he wanted to stop over to talk. When he arrived, I was shaking like a leaf in fear of what he was going to tell me. The first question he asked was what happened to the baby. I told him with tears in my eyes that I had a miscarriage in the third month. He then told me he would like to see me because he really liked me, and that this discussion should end. I was so happy I wanted to kiss him, but I did not dare. We watched a few TV shows, and he went home. I was relieved he understood, and we could put this behind us.

I still had the problem of finding a place to live. Rents were so expensive when trying to survive on a teacher's salary. Time was running out on the lease and Gail was getting nervous about me finding a place. Nick was calling regularly to see whether I found a place. The following Thursday he invited me to dinner and told me his lease was also coming due. He then asked me if we could share the apartment I was living in because the apartment had two bedrooms and was furnished by Gail. I asked him if he was sure before I approached Gail about the furniture. He said he was sure, and I should check with her.

The next day I called Gail and asked her if she would leave the furniture. She asked me whether Nick had furniture and I told him he had rented a furnished apartment that he was living in when he went to college. She also asked me if I told Nick about being Pregnant and I told her yes. She then told me she would leave the furniture and make sure Nick's name was also on the lease. She also told me Nick and I should go to the rental office to secure a lease. We ended up keeping the apartment.

Moving day for Nick was on the first of the month and I helped him to move. After two years living together, Nick asked my father for my hand in marriage and then he proposed to me. I said yes and we were married four months later. Gail gave us an ocean cruise as a wedding gift. Nick and I ended up having three children in the coming years. Two boys and a girl. We were totally happy and spent some forty-nine years together. We traveled and attended every sport our children were involved in. We would spend endless hours talking about the time we went to college and the movies we had seen. Nick would kid me about how many times we have seen the same gangster movies. It was like most marriages that had ups and downs. All those years I would still think of mysterious Dan, Tony and Paul who had a father that was a gangster and Joel that most likely became a well-known doctor. Our children would get married and make us grandparents. I enjoyed being a grandmother because I could spoil them and send them home.

All through my marriage I would write short stories about women's traits and in some cases their attraction to gangsters. I had some published and gave a few classes about women identifying themselves with gangsters. I would have occasional dreams about Nick being part of the mob. I would wake up in a cold sweat and fight off being guilty. I think some days I was totally caught up daydreaming about gangsters.

This was the time in my life I needed to prove that traits were in the eyes of the woman. Dan was so positive in his thinking it was difficult for me to ignore his beliefs. The struggle was how could I prove or disapprove this Dan's belief. I started looking into my friends' eyes and tried to tie that into one of Dan's five traits. I happened to notice my friend named Alice that had an abundance of social skills. Her eyes were always sparkling. Then there was Tammy, the great defender of those that had problems. Her eyes were telling me she had an abundance of empathy. She always looked like her eyes were close to crying. And then there was

Mary who was always into self-improvement and who had big blue eyes. Sally was my neighbor who always had to say something humorous. Her eyes always seemed to be blinking as if she was looking for the next thing to say funny. My other neighbor had self-awareness because she was always staring you down. Maybe Dan was right, and you could determine a trait looking at your eyes. My final test would be on myself. Why was I so interested in gangsters? I looked closely in the mirror, and I realized my eyes seemed to get bigger when I mentioned the word gangster.

This would start me looking at everyone's eyes whether I was at the grocery store or shopping at the mall. I have to say I received a lot of strange looks. I would keep track of my findings if I could see them do something that would represent that trait. I would gather at least five hundred examples.

This would be the format for my book, which would allow me to do numerous seminars on the subject. The book ended up being a best seller. I had dreams that half the women in the country were looking into their eyes trying to determine what trait they were. I was hoping Dan was still alive to thank him for all the information he gave me on women traits. I was also interviewed by a local TV station to talk about the book. The royalties from the book would allow us to purchase a condo in Florida to spend the winters.

Nick was right about one thing, I loved gangster movies. In fact, I would watch them over and over again. I was proud of myself maturing from an insecure young girl to this proud mother with children and grandchildren. I would remember the holidays singing Christmas carols and exchanging gifts. We would enjoy getting our families together while preparing wonderful meals. We would age gracefully over the years always looking out for each year.

Nick would pass away when he was seventy-two and I would be left with grief and being on my own. Nick always took care of the finances and most things around the house. I am now trying to figure out how to put a nail into the wall to hang a picture or trying to balance my checkbook. I think of all the things I took for granite. In the old days, children stayed close to home. Now they work all over the country. Every day I think of downsizing to a place that has an association responsible for lawn maintenance and snow removal. I caught myself looking at homes in senior citizen developments in the Sunday Newspaper. Each time I would find an excuse not to go look at the houses that were on sale. I would think how I could leave all the memories and how my children would feel. I knew down deep I had to move to be on one floor and have people my age to associate with. I finally found a place that offered everything that I needed, and I put my house up for sale. The children were not overly excited about me moving. The idea of being alone and dismantling a home we lived in for thirty-five years was a daunting experience. I would work twelve-hour days sorting things out to take, discard or pass off to the children. Children today do not want the cherished collections that we loved so much. The house was sold and moving day arrived. The movers arrived and quickly emptied the house with my precious belongings. As I was backing out of the driveway, I remembered the happy and sad memories living in that house. I stopped for a second just to stare at the house and remember the children playing in the front yard. I arrived at my new residence before the movers came. They must have stopped for coffee. I went in to check the pieces of tape I put on the floor where I wanted to put the pieces of furniture. This house was smaller than my other home and I had limited storage. I would have to discard more items because there was no place to put them.

CHAPTER 8

The next day the neighbors came one at a time and introduced themselves. Some brought cookies, flowers and cards. These were wonderful thoughtful people. Some were widows like me, and some were still married to their loved ones. These types of homes were always going up for sale. I got new neighbors and new opportunities to talk to about our lives and memories. Although we would get together occasionally, I missed not getting together more often. One of my neighbors would plan monthly dinners at local restaurants, which was something to look forward to. After I lived here a few years this neighbor moved, and dinners no longer existed.

A house was sold up the street to a couple that downsized like I had done. When I first met David the man of the house, there was something reminded me of someone. He was strictly confidential and talked about his experiences in life. He would say something and if you asked him a question you would not get an answer. As I got to know the family, he was between the Great Gatsby and my acquaintance Dan. There was something very mysterious about him. We loved to hear his stories and jokes. He enjoyed having you walk into a punch line he had created. He made us laugh. He always had parties and simple gatherings. He met more people from all walks of life. He would keep groups separate for some reason. I finally surmised if he got everybody together you be able to find out more about him. I remember complaining about something that may not be a problem. He said, "do not scratch where you do not itch". He would always make you welcome, feel good about yourself and help you whenever he could. Here I was fifty years later trying to figure out how to ask questions to learn more about this guy like I did when I knew Dan.

He and his wife were always having parties at their house for different groups of people. His wife was having medical problems which caused him to do most things around the house. He was extremely positive in trying to make her better.

I ended up selling the condo in Florida because it was getting more difficult to travel back and forth and the neighbors were not as friendly as my neighbors at home. This was a tremendous effort on my part to be alone and try to dismantle the condo and to disperse all the furniture and the items we accumulated over the years. I finally sold the condo and ended up going back home. I thanked the neighbors that called and texted me while I was getting the condo ready to sell. Those communications made me feel wonderful about the development I lived in.

The more I lived in this development the more I loved it. In fact, I hated to go away for an extended period of time. I was still trying to live on my own and finish the grieving process. My neighbors were helping me to move on. A few gentlemen would ask me out but, in most cases, they bored me. Gail's husband passed away a few years ago and left her wealthy. Except for not having any children, she seemed to be happy. I thought I would write a book on my life in the fast lane. This book would be totally fiction because I never witnessed the fast lane. I mentioned to David it would be nice to have a male friend to hang around with. He looked at me with a puzzled look on his face and as usual never said a word.

About a week later, David arranged a telephone call with me, and a guy named Mike. Although I thought this was strange, it was typical of David. I would find out later Mike would change my life. First of all, he would take me to the fantastic places to eat dinner and take me to the theater. He was also like my neighbor David, he knew everybody. He was sophisticated, smart and fun to be with. He was another person that you would not get away with asking him questions. He was romantic and would buy me flowers for no reason. We were the same age and had little interest in living together or getting married. Some of the women in the neighborhood were jealous and wanted David to fix them up with a guy. He would shy away of introducing men to them. I could not figure this out because he knew so many people. I think he knew I liked gangsters.

As time went on, we were inseparable doing things like most couples watching TV, taking long walks and laughing. He would make comments that I looked vivacious. Even my friends were saying the same thing. It was one thing when he said it, but when my friends said it made me feel warm and fuzzy. He liked to make fun of me in a positive way which I thought was cute. One day he mentioned if something would happen to him, I needed to call David and go with him to his place and take the suitcase from under the bed and drop it off at the address on the top side of the suitcase. I asked if he was in some kind of trouble. Of course, I never got an answer. He told me please do this one favor for me. I could not sleep that night because I was falling in love with him and was concerned about him and getting involved with something that was not legal. Over the following months, I dismissed what he told me, and Mike and I enjoyed the things we did together.

I went to see David and asked him point blank what Mike was involved in. He looked at me with a long stare and commented you are better off not knowing. That sent chills down my spine.

What is it with these guys? Everything is a secret and confidential. As I left his house, I decided I would talk to Mike and if I could not get an answer, I would break up with him. I called Gail and she told me she was coming to town to visit her stepdaughter. I told her I needed to talk to her and get her opinion. She told me she would call me when she got in and let me know when we could have dinner.

I kept thinking about all the strange things Mike and I had witnessed over the past two years. For example, when we were at the mall and we ran into David, they pretended they did not know each other. He did tell me that if anything happened to him, I should call David to go with me to his house to retrieve the suitcase. If David did not know Mike, how did he arrange for us two to meet? The more I thought about things that happened over the past two years, the more I got a little scared. I kept hanging out with Mike over the following weeks trying to figure this out and try to get answers to my concerns.

The following week, I met Gail for lunch and told her my concerns about Mike. Gail made a comment that maybe I was reading too much into what Mike does for a living. She also made a comment regarding how I liked gangsters, and this may be driving me to make assumptions. She was no help, and I changed the discussion to sister talk. Like have you been seeing anybody lately or have you bought any new clothes? The truth of the matter is I preferred talking about Mike and what he was involved in. My sister and I hugged, and we left the restaurant. Maybe Dan was right all along, you cannot change a women's trait no matter how hard you try. I was enthused about gangsters and what they did. That may be the reason I was attracted to Mike. This may be the reason I was trying to find out what he did for a living. I may have wanted Mike to be part of the mob.

Christmas was a few days away and my children were arriving to stay the week. I could only have a few people stay at the house because I only had one extra bedroom, so I rented rooms at a local motel for the rest of them to stay. The holidays were wonderful to see my children and their loved ones. I enjoyed playing games with my grandchildren. It was crowded at Christmas dinner, but we had fun. I invited Mike to meet my family and enjoy the festivities. They all told me later they liked him. My oldest son was aways suspicious of everyone and did not seem to get a clear answer to what Mike did for a living when he worked. To be truthful, I did not know what he did for a living either and I did not care.

In the following days and weeks after Christmas, Mike was acting very strange. In fact, we stopped in the mall to take Christmas gifts back to the store. Mike saw somebody at the mall that caused him to want to leave the mall immediately. I thought this was very strange because we had talked about having Chinese at the mall. He dropped me off at the house and left. I knew there was something on his mind. I did not hear from him for about a week. This was not unusual because he had gone for periods of time like this before. He called to apologize and said he was on a business trip. In the upcoming days we would go out to dinner, he would always ask me to drive, which I thought was strange.

It was Thursday and it was the coldest day in February. My nextdoor neighbor called and asked me to turn on the TV to see the news. There was a car bombing and the person killed was Mike. They said it was mob killing. My chest was hurting, and I had a tough time breathing. I was crying out loud. I loved everything about Mike then I remembered about the suitcase under his bed. I called David about Mike being murdered and asked him to escort me to Mike's house. I used the key he gave me to enter the house and I found the suitcase under the bed. I gave the suitcase to David and drove to the location he told me to go. I did not see him look at the address. Somehow, he knew the address without looking at the case. When we got there David went into the house and he came out empty handed. I thought it was strange that Mike would ask me to have David escort to the house. Maybe David would be there to protect me.

The following day I was looking for information regarding Mike's funeral. In fact, there was no mention of a funeral in the weeks to come. Once again, I was lost and bored over the next week. My son called me to tell me he told me to watch this guy. Here the shoe was on the other foot. When he was a child, I would caution him about hanging around boys that got in trouble. Somehow, he was enjoying this change.

CHAPTER 9

The first day in March, my doorbell rang and when I opened the door there were two well-dressed men that introduced their selves as FBI agents. They immediately showed me their identification and asked if they could come into the house. I could tell they were looking around the front room. I asked them to sit down. They started to question me about Mike. I explained we were friends and socialized together going to movies and dinners. They asked how much I knew about Mike. I told them he was a confidential person that talked very little about himself. Did he ever ask you to do something for him? Yes, he told me if anything happened to him, I should go to his house and take a suitcase from underneath his bed and deliver it to the address on the suitcase. Was anybody with you? Yes, my neighbor David. Mike asked me to take him with me. Where does this neighbor live? He lives four houses up on the same side of the street from my house. When we got to the location to drop off the suitcase my neighbor took it into the house and came out. We drove to our homes and parted. Did this neighbor tell you anything? He only mentioned that he felt bad I lost a good friend. Then they asked me if they could search the house. I told them that it was okay. I was now getting concerned and I wanted to call David to have him tell his side of the story.

They finished their search, and I told them to talk to my neighbor about the suitcase. They said the house was empty and the neighbors said they moved out in the middle of the night. They told me they would get back to me to look at mug shots to identify my neighbor. I was dumbfounded and mad how I could get involved with these type people. Sometimes it is just better to look and not touch. Was I set up or just happened to be there? Whatever it was, I missed Mike and David. I was not going to mention to my neighbors about the visit from the FBI. My son was calling me every day for an update, and I did not tell him either.

The following day, I received a telephone call from a lady who identified herself as Mike's daughter. She told me he had left me something and I promised to deliver it to you. Plus, I wanted to meet you because my father talked so much about you. I was tempted to hang up, but I was wondering what Mike had left me. First of all. I did not know if Mike had a daughter or if this person was his daughter. Maybe, she was going to kill me because they thought I knew too much. I told her I would meet her in a restaurant with my sister. She agreed and we set a date to meet the following Friday at Dino's restaurant. I was also looking forward to meeting her to get some answers about her father. Maybe she could explain what he did in his life and why he was murdered.

Gail and I went to Dino's that Friday at noon and ordered a glass of wine. This young lady walked in with a package with a bow on it. She was beautiful and elegantly dressed in a New York style dress. She walked up to the table and introduced herself as Tammy and said she recognized me from the pictures my father took of me. You know he loved you very much, but he wanted to protect you from his personal life. She told me she did not know what was in the package, but he made me promise that I would deliver it to you. Gail jumped right into the discussion and asked her what her father did. This was Gail, get to the facts. My father was in the mob, and he became an informer. He was really a very nice guy and a great father. Gail asked about her mother and Tammy told her she passed away when I was ten. Gail asked about the rest of the family. We were the only ones left in the family. We did have an uncle we called Dan, but he died many years ago. I asked if Dan was an author and she said he was, but he used an assumed name. I was totally taken back about Mike being Dan's nephew. All at once I got this warm feeling throughout my whole body. I told her the story of Dan and how he helped me out when I was your age. Tammy announced she had to catch a plane to go back to New York. I thanked her and hugged her. Gail told me she really liked Tammy and I should call her once in a while. I caught Tammy by the door and asked if she knew if Mike had a friend named David. She told me she had never heard her father mention a friend named David. I was not sure she was telling me the truth. I left the restaurant with the package.

When I got home the two FBI agents were waiting for me and wanted to know what was in the package. I told them I did not know but they were welcome to open it. They opened the package and there was a letter and pictures of Mike and me and a beautiful ring. I asked them if they wanted to take the package and they said no. When they left, I said to myself these two are going to be following me forever. We may even end up being good friends. They must have followed me to Dino's and are probably ease dropping on my phone.

The following week an FBI agent called and said they would send a vehicle to pick me up to take me to their office to look at mug shots. They asked me what a good day would be for me. I told the agent Wednesday was a good day and he told me they would pick me up at nine o'clock. I asked if I should bring anything with me.

He said no but just plans to spend at least four hours at our office. On Wednesday two agents picked me up. There was one woman and a man. I tried to start a conversation, but I found out they were not interested in small talk. When we entered the building, I was taken to a conference room loaded with mechanical devices. There were cameras, recording devices, a large screen, projector and other mechanical devices I did not recognize.

Three people entered the room and started to fiddle with the equipment. Pictures of people began to appear on the large screen. The young lady operating the projector, which was actually a commuter, asked the other two people where they wanted to start. The one man asked me how old did I think this neighbor was? I told him about seventy years old. They scanned pictures of men in that age bracket. After two hours of searching, I said that was my neighbor. They then switched to a sub file which would tell them all about this person. They immediately shut down the commuter and escorted me out of the room. Then they told me they were taking me Home. They thanked me and the same two agents drove me home. Once in the vehicle I asked who was my neighbor? I did not get an answer.

When I got home, I was totally confused thinking about my neighbor and who he was. I wanted to know more about him and whether I would ever see him again. My neighbors quickly ran over to ask me about the black vehicle that picked me up this morning. This was the type of place everybody knows everything about everyone. I told them as much as I could because I knew very little. It was amazing listening to them about how they all suspected something was strange about him. It was like an old saying about being a Monday Morning Quarterback. The days would pass, and I was beginning to forget about the ordeal. I missed Mike and the fun we had. I was once again bored and lonely trying to think about things to do. I always enjoyed talking to men and now there was nobody.

I thought of David living in another place having parties and making everyone feel good about themselves. I also wondered if he would ever tell his new neighbors who he really was. I would be forever thankful he somehow arranged for me to meet Mike. I will always keep wondering how the two knew each other. Once again, if only I could ask a few questions. If I had one dream, I would like to have Mike, David, Paul and Dan in the same room to answer all my questions.

About two weeks later, my neighbor brought over a small package that was sent to me with her address on it. When I opened the package there was a cell phone and a letter with instructions in it. The letter was from David which said I will call you on Wednesday at 10am. Please go into your vehicle and make sure the windows are closed. I will call to talk to you. Please take this note and tear it up in small pieces and flush it down the toilet immediately. After I talk to you, please discard this burner phone in one of the lakes in the development. Make sure nobody sees you. This was typical of David sending mail out to a person with a different address. Maybe I will ask him why he did that.

I was trembling thinking of what would happen if those agents broke down my door and took the note and the phone. I immediately ran to the bathroom and tore the note up in small pieces and flushed them down the toilet. I took the phone and wrapped it in plastic and put it in a coffee maker I never used. I was so excited that I would be able to find out more about Mike and him. Maybe this is why women get so excited about gangsters. The challenge of always trying to find out what is happening with the mob. Although I was afraid to talk to my neighbor, I needed to know more about Mike and his connection to Mike.

The only thing I was worried about was being accused of aiding and abetting a criminal and ending up going to jail. I could not sleep at night thinking about the telephone call and what my neighbor would tell me.

CHAPTER 10

It was Monday and the sun was shining but still cold outside. The only thing I could think about was the call I would receive on Wednesday. My son called and we talked a little and he said I sounded a little nervous. I told him I had a slight cold and was trying to stay warm. I finally realized I enjoyed the suspense and the thought of living on the edge. This trait of idealizing gangsters was a reality and here I was smack in the middle of it.

After Mike's daughter explained to me about her father and what he did, I turned my attention to my neighbor, whatever his real name was. Who moves out of his house in the middle of the night. What about the suitcase he said he left at the address marked on the case. Why was the FBI looking for him? What was in the writing below his mug shot that I was not allowed to see. So many unanswered questions, but I had to admit I loved every second of it.

After my husband Nick Passed away, life in general was boring. Here I was older and facing the same issues as all people do at my age. When Mike came into my life, everything was exciting and something to look forward to. Now the most exciting thing in my life was waiting for a phone call from the mysterious neighbor which everyone adored. As I look back, he made everyone laugh and involved us in fun things like small trips and parties. Now he was gone also.

The days, hours and minutes seemed to drag on. I unwrapped

the burner phone from my hiding spot and kept it in the bedroom. Wednesday finally arrived and I patiently waited until 9:45am and

I went into my car in the garage and made sure the windows were closed just as he asked me to do. I was nervous and my hands were shaking as I watched the clock in my car tick away. I pulled the piece of paper out of my pocket that had the questions I had written down. I read the questions once again to make sure I did not miss anything I wanted to ask. I missed one question regarding the suitcase under Mike's Bed. I wanted to know what was in that suitcase because it brought the FBI to my door.

At ten o'clock, the burner phone rang and a voice on the other end of the phone said, "Lee are you alone". I answered in a shaky voice, This is Lee and I am alone. Lee, I wanted to talk to you and thank you for being nice to my friend Mike. I am so sorry about Mike being killed. I know you have numerous questions you would like to ask me. I must remind you I have limited time to spend on this phone. We always call you David. Is that your real name? No, it is not my real name, but I cannot tell you my real name. What was your connection to Mike? We were childhood Friends. We grew up in mob families. Mike was a nephew of Dan, and I was a younger brother to Paul. We have seen you a few times at parties at my father and mother's house. Why is everything so secretive? You have to realize when you are associated with a mob family you really cannot tell anybody about yourself or the family. After we grew up and graduated from college, I became a lawyer and Mike became a CPA. We were recruited by our families to enter the family business. Either one of us wanted that type of life.

To make the story short, we both got into trouble and Mike went to jail and I ended up with a suspended sentence. Mike became a witness for the FBI and was released from jail and entered the federal witness protection program. He was given a new name, address and social security number. Numerous gangsters went to jail after he testified. He was definitely a marked man. He did meet a woman and got married and ended up with a daughter. There was a contract on him, but they could not find him. Mike called me a few years ago to help him out. This was strictly for financial reasons.

When I moved into the development and had parties you looked very familiar to me. After I questioned you a few times about your past, I realized you were the girl that my brother Paul brought to my father and mother's parties. I knew talking to Mike's uncle years ago you were fascinated by gangsters. This is when I decided to arrange Mike to meet you. This way I could keep track of Mike because I knew you could be trusted. I want to apologize to you for my actions. I think it worked out because you two fell in love.

My next question was what was in the suitcase? He told me it was a half million dollars that was going to be delivered to his daughter in New York. Mike wanted to make sure his daughter was taken care of. I told David his daughter came to see me. I was surprised he never told me about his daughter. He was only protecting you. The less you knew the better you were off.

The gangs are relentless in finding people like Mike and me. It is a family thing. They will spend endless time searching for those that become a federal witness and make an example of them. It goes with the territory.

Why are you on the run? I also did what Mike did by becoming a federal witness, but I did not accept the federal witness protection program. Not doing so, the FBI tries to watch every move I make. How do you survive? Mike and I stole enough money from our organizations to live a good life. Will I ever see you again? This is the last conversation we will ever have. Do me one favor, do not mention this conversation to anyone. I will now hang up and please throw the phone in one of those ponds. David, we all mis you and I hope that you find happiness in the future. Goodbye.

I was glad he answered my questions, but I was heartbroken because I missed Mike and hurt, I would never see David again. I felt so alone and lost thinking of all the memories I had over the years. The mistakes I made and my wonderful husband, my children and my grandchildren. Maybe Dan was right about women who are drawn to the gangster type guys. There may not be a place for a woman to exist in that environment which I surmised was a lonely life. I existed each day of my life remembering all the memories of my family and the people I met over the years. I missed my husband Nick and my relationships with Mike, David, Dan, Paul and the many wonderful neighbors I have. I would sit in the sunroom and think about David and where he was right now. An unusual character that made everybody happy. I miss that association and the research I used to do on women's traits.

As the years went by, I would spend my time trying to find David but without a name it was not likely to happen. One of my neighbors moved to Phoenix to get out of the cold weather. We would talk once a month exchanging information on our neighbors, recipes and scuttlebutt about our families. She called me in the middle of the month in June and she told me about an ex-gangster that was murdered. She also said it looked like David. I asked her to send me a picture and sure enough it was David. I was heart sick thinking back of all the memories. I guess he was right when he told me on the phone the mob was not forgiving. That would be the end of my research trying to find him. There was nothing left of the old gang but everlasting memories.

I am still attending neighborhood functions, but it is not the same. I am now spending more time with my grandchildren and reading novels and of course gangster stories. I think a lot about my husband and things we did over the years. My children were all doing well and spending time with their friends making memories. I see my children once in a while and spend a little time with my sister. She still makes fun of me and my attraction to gangsters and always tells me I watch too many movies like the Godfather. I guess the movies spark my memories of some of the great times I had. Sometimes I think I was living on the edge of life.

I still remember what Dan told me that the trait of a women lies in her eyes. I knew when I looked into the mirror it told me a lot particularly when I thought of gangsters. There was this smile and my eyes sparkled. He also told me that gangsters care about their community and live by their own rules that include honor and conduct. I think I was the luckiest women in the world to live two lives with fantastic memories. I guess I was told many times the only thing you have are your memories.

The End

Printed in the United States
by Baker & Taylor Publisher Services